日本女性2人詩集（1）

おばさんから子どもたちへ
贈る詩の花束

Collected Coupling Poems of Japanese Two Women Poets
In English & Japanese (Vol.1)

From Aunties to Children
A Gift Of A Bouquet of Poems

新川和江・水崎野里子

Kazue Shinkawa & Noriko Mizusaki

ブックウェイ

新川和江詩集：目次
Collected Poems of Kazue Shinkawa : Contents

おうち　*Your Home* ⋯⋯⋯⋯⋯⋯⋯⋯⋯⋯⋯⋯⋯ *6*

捜す　*Searching* ⋯⋯⋯⋯⋯⋯⋯⋯⋯⋯⋯⋯⋯⋯ *8*

歌　*A Song* ⋯⋯⋯⋯⋯⋯⋯⋯⋯⋯⋯⋯⋯⋯⋯ *10*

お天気がよいので　*In a Fine Weather* ⋯⋯⋯⋯⋯⋯ *12*

野原のポプラ　*A Popular in a Field* ⋯⋯⋯⋯⋯⋯ *14*

鬼ごっこ　*A Tag Game* ⋯⋯⋯⋯⋯⋯⋯⋯⋯⋯ *16*

橋をわたる時　*Crossing a Bridge* ⋯⋯⋯⋯⋯⋯ *18*

ちいさな川は　*A Tiny Stream...* ⋯⋯⋯⋯⋯⋯⋯ *20*

『火へのオード 18』より　*From Ode to Fire 18* ⋯⋯⋯⋯ *22*

水崎野里子詩集：目次
Collected Poems of Noriko Mizusaki : Contents

おうち　*Home*･･ *28*

ひまわりへのオード　*Ode to the Sunflower*　･･････････････････ *30*

夏祭り　*Summer Festival* ･･･････････････････････････････ *32*

ガンジスの黎明　*Dawn; The Ganges* ･･････････････････････ *34*

お月さま　*Moon Watching Festival* ･･････････････････････ *38*

春　*Spring* ･･･ *42*

力一杯走っていこう　*Go Dash As Hard As You Can*･････････ *44*

風車^{かざぐるま}　*Windmill in a Toy*･･････････････････････････ *46*

かたち　*Shapes* ･･･････････････････････････････････････ *48*

ヒロシマの折り鶴　*Paper Cranes in Hiroshima* ･･････････ *50*

言葉の花束：終わりに
　A Bouquet of Poems to you : After Words ･････････････ *52*

謝辞　*Words of Gratitude* ･･･････････････････････････ *54*

新川和江

Kazue Shinkawa

おうち

ただいま　とかえってゆくと
おかえりなさい　って
やさしい声が　きこえるところ

ストーブがもえていて
おなべの中で
シチューがことこと　にえているところ

おてあらいがあって
おふろがあって
へいきで　はだかになれるところ

おし入れがあって
たんすがあって
わたしがお宮まいりにきたきものなどが
いまでもだいじに　しまわれているところ

夜ねむると　おかあさんが
（ときどきは　おとうさんもね）
おやすみ　いいゆめをごらん　と
おふとんをなおしに　きてくださるところ

Your Home

Is a place when you say "I'm home!"
"Welcome home!" there
A gentle voice you can hear

A place where a stove is burning
In a pan
Some stew is simmering

A place where there is a wash room
There is a bath room
Not in hesitation you can be naked

A place where there are closets
There are chests
My old kimono robes on my shrine visitations
Put in so cherished even now

A place when you sleep at night your mom
(Sometimes your dad as well)
Comes down there to adjust your futon covers
" Good night. Have a nice dream" mom would say

(Translator: Noriko Mizusaki)

捜す

わたしは誰のあばらなのでしょう
わたしの元の場所は　どこなのでしょう
日が暮れかかるのに
まだ　見つからない

川が流れています　わたしの中を
みなもとは　どの山奥にあるのでしょう
せせらぎの音がつよくなるので
さかのぼって　行かずにはいられません

暗くなっても　家に帰ってこない
ついに帰ってこない　女の子がいるものです
捜さないでください　彼女自身がいま
＜捜すひと＞に　なっているのですから

Searching

Whose rib on the earth am I?
Where is my place of the origin?
It is getting dark into the evening
I have not searched out yet

A river is flowing in my mind
Which heart of the mountains has the source?
The rustling I hear get stronger and stronger
I cannot stop tracing back to the source: upstream

Some girl will not return even after dark
She will not eventually: by any means come back
Do not search for her: she has turned now herself
A searching person

(Translator: Noriko Mizusaki)

歌

はじめての子を持ったとき
女のくちびるから
ひとりでに洩れだす歌は
この世でいちばん優しい歌だ
それは　遠くで
荒れて　逆立っている　海のたてがみをも
おだやかに宥めてしまう
星々を　うなずかせ
旅びとを　振りかえらせ
風にも忘れられた　さびしい谷間の
痩せたリンゴの木の枝にも
あかい　灯をともす
おお　そうでなくて
なんで子どもが育つだろう
この　いたいけな
無防備なものが

A Song

When a woman had a first child
A song that leaks out of her lips by itself is
The most gentle song in this world
It will calm down
Even the manes of the far sea
Rough and the bristles up
Let stars nod
Let travelers look back
Set red tiny lamps on
The branches of the lean apple tree
In the lonesome valley: even a wind
Might have lost the memory
Oh! Unless it is
How will a child grow up?
This tiny one so dear
Defenseless

(Translator: Noriko Mizusaki)

お天気がよいので

あまり　お天気がよいので
すみずみまで照らしだされて
この世は
よく磨かれた鏡のうちがわのようだ
どこかに
あるらしい　もっとたしかな現実を
素直にうつして　たんぽぽが咲く
そっくりおなじく　柳の枝が風に揺れる
そこここで　人が死ぬ
さようならと
わたしが恋人にお辞儀をする
横断歩道を渡ってゆく
やはり　振り返らずに

In a Fine Weather

Today is too fine a weather
Even corners are shined out
This world looks like
The inside part of a mirror polished well
Somewhere else
There might be more certain the reality
Reflecting it simple dandelions bloom out
Just the same willows' branches sway in a wind
Here and there people are passing away
Good bye!
I bowed to my love
I walk across the crossway
Just the same not looking back

(Translator: Noriko Mizusaki)

野原のポプラ

若いポプラが
野原にいっぽん立っている
つよい風が　吹き倒そうとするけれど
倒れるわけにはいかないのです
またらいねんも　この木の下で会おうねと
少年と少女がやくそくしたのを
ポプラはしっかり聞いたから

はげしい雨が　葉を落とそうとするけれど
おとすわけにはいかないのです
ことしはじめて　巣をかけた小鳥が
小さなたまごを
だいじにだいじに温めているさいちゅうだから

少しかしいで　それでも倒れず
若いポプラはいっしょけんめい立っている
またらいねんも会おうねと
やくそくしたのは
このぼくです　というように
やがてかえる小鳥のひなのおとうさんは
このぼくです　というように

風のない日も
ヒラヒラ　ヒラヒラ　葉をそよがせて
青空に　白い雲のひかる日には
キラキラ　キラキラ　葉をかがやかせて

A Popular in a Field

A young poplar is standing
alone in the field.
A strong wind tries to blow it down but
it cannot fall to the ground
because it surely heard that
a young couple promised to meet
next year again under its branches.

Heavy rain tries to tear its leaves off but
it cannot shed them
because a bird having nested its first year in it
is now sitting on tiny eggs
it so cherishes.

Tilting a little but not falling down
the young poplar is standing up as strongly as it can
as if it promised to meet again next year
as if it is the daddy of the young birds
soon to be hatched.

Even on windless days
its leaves dance up and down
and on days with clear blue skies
and dazzling white clouds
its leaves shine bright, so bright.

(Translated by Noriko Mizusaki)

鬼ごっこ

「あなたは霧？風？それともけむり？」
苦しまぎれに呼びかけると
遠くのほうから
あのひとのこえがかえって来た
「あなたは霧？風？それともけむり？」

なんという　間の抜けた
さびしい鬼ごっこ！
わたしたちはどちらも目隠しをして
相手をつかまえようと
漠漠とした霧の中に
手ばかりむなしく泳がせているのだった

「あなたが　いっぽんの木であればいい
そうすればつかまって泣くことも出来るのに！」
苦しまぎれに呼びかけると
じきそばで
あのひとの声がした
「あなたが　いっぽんの木であればいい
そうすれば伐り倒すことお出来るのに！」

A Tag Game

"Are you mist? A wind? Or a smoke?"
I shouted out driven into a tight plight
Then from a far direction
The tagger's voice returned to me
"Are you mist? A wind? Or a smoke?"

What a silly and
Pitiful tag game!
Both of us wearing blindfolds
Stretching our searching hands
Out in the vast mist
To catch each opponent in vain

"I wish you were a tree!
Then clinging to you I can weep!"
In my poor plight I shouted to another tag
When close to me the voice was heard
"I wish you were a tree
Then I could axe you down'

(Translator: Noriko Mizusaki)

橋をわたる時

向ふ岸には
いい村がありさうです
心のやさしいひとが
待ってゐてくれそうです
のどかに牛が啼いて
れんげ畠は
いつでも花ざかりのやうです

いいことがありさうです
ひとりでに微笑まれてきます
何だか　かう
急ぎ足になります

Crossing a Bridge

On the opposite shore
There might be a good village
A gentle-minded person is
Likely waiting for me
Peacefully cows cry moo
A field of Chinese milk vetches
Looks in the prime of flowers any time

There might be good things
I smile to myself
Somehow I don't know
I hurry my steps

(Translator: Noriko Mizusaki)

ちいさな川は…

ちいさな川は
一日中　うたっている
鳥が　はすかいに
つい！　ととべば　鳥のうたを
白い雲がかげをおとせば　霧のうたを
風が川面を吹いてわたれば　風のうたを
女の子が花を浮かべれば　花のうたを
夜がくれば　空いっぱいの星たちのうたを

A Tiny Stream…

A tiny brook is
Singing all day long
When a bird happens to
Fly over it askew
A song of the bird
When white clouds drop shadows
A song of mist
When a wind blows across it
A song of the wind
When a girl floats a flower
A song of the flower
When a night comes
A song of stars full in the sky

(Translator: Noriko Mizusaki)

『火へのオード18』より

14

火はひそんでいた
戸袋の陰や　梁のうえ　濡れ縁の下　物置の隅に
そうして昼も夜も
同族の意志が一挙に凝るのを待ちうけていた
火は狭苦しい屋根の下で
ひと掴みの豆を煮るためにのみ　下婢のように
人間に使役され続けてきた自分の歴史が気に喰わなかった
火は人間よりもむしろ神に近い
おのれの高貴性を信じて疑わなかったから
折あらば本来の地位を奪還しようと狙っていた
えたいの知れぬ情熱が
火を極度にたかぶらせた或る夜
戸袋の陰から　梁のうえから　濡れ縁の下から　物置の隅から
火は一斉に鬨の声をあげ　結集し
同族を支配し続けてきた人間の住居の一を
またたく間に舐り尽くして占拠した

火はますます勢いを得て
隣りの家にも　その隣りの家にも手を伸ばしていった
人間が言う＜ささやかな幸福＞などは
火にとってはひと振りの調味料に過ぎなかった
火は積年の飢餓を満たすべく
貪り食い　食い漁った

火は知らなかった　自分の姿が
限度を知らず肥大し　成長してゆく
世にもまがまがしいけだものの様相を呈していることを
ひとつの町を恐怖の底につき落として
火は咆哮し
背中の毛を天にもとどけと　逆立てた

From Ode to Fire 18

14

Fire was lurking
Behind shutter cases: on beams: under open verandahs and in the corner of
barns
Day and night
He was waiting for his clans to set unified in the desires
He hated his history which had been long forced to work by humans
They treated him like a female slave only for cooking a handful of beans
In a small sooty kitchen
Fire is closer to a god than a human
He did not pose a question to the nobleness of his own
So he sought for the good occasion to restore his original status
One night when strange passion caused him extreme excitement
From behind shutter cases: from on beams: from under open verandahs: and
from corners of barns
Fire came escaped and raising up war cries all together he gathered himself
in unification
He occupied one of the dwellings of humans and in a moment licked it out
Humans had been too dominating over him

Fire was gaining his force more and more
Stretching his hands to the next house and then to the next to it
Such a motto as "small happiness" humans might say was
Just a one bit of the seasonings to him
He devoured and scavenged for his foods
To satisfy his hunger and starvation for these long years

Fire did not know he came to look like a most weird beast in the world
Gaining weights with no ends to go swell bigger and bigger
Pushing one city to drop to the bottom of terror
Fire howled

遠巻きにした水の砲列が射撃を開始した
火のけだものは　よろめいては起ち上がり　また起ち上がり
悶え　のたうち回るうちに　ついに力尽き
みるみる白毛の老いさらばえた姿となって　這い蹲った
腹の下に
逃げおくれた若い人妻とその幼な子を抱えこんで

人間は号泣した　しかし火もまた無念の涙を流した
黒焦げの醜い残骸をさらしたのみで　革命は成らなかった
爛れた空が白みはじめる頃
火はおのれの情熱のおぞましい膨張をおのれの高貴な魂に愧じて
すごすごと身をひそませて帰っていった
手近な家の
戸袋の陰　梁のうえ　濡れ縁の下　物置の隅に

Bristled his hair on the back high up to the heaven

Cannons of water started their shots from far positions
Fire the beast stumbled down and rose up again and again
In agony turning around and writhing he wasted all his force
Turning himself quickly into a figure old and aged with white hair
He went crawling on the ground with his limbs
Under the belly holding a young mother and her baby
They could not escape from him

Humans cried out loud but Fire also shed his tears in regrets
Only having exposed the ugly body scorched black he had no success in
revolution
Around when the festered sky started to be lighted
He started to come back home to hide himself in dejection
Feeling ashamed of the pitiful expansion of his passion in his noble soul
He came back to: behind shutter cases: on beams: under open verandahs and
in the corners of barns
In your houses nearby

(Translator: Noriko Mizusaki)

水崎野里子

Noriko Mizusaki

おうち

あなた　ほんの小さいときに
病気になって一ヶ月入院したの
覚えている？
病院であなた言い続けた

おうちに帰りたいって
退院してあなたおうちに帰った
あなたきょろきょろ見回していた
この部屋の中　覚えている？

炉端もマントルピースもない
おうち
でも
おうちよ

ごめんね　お母さん
お掃除さぼって
でも覚えていてね　あなた
「おうちに帰る！」って言った

エアコンあるけど
けちって
お布団かけて
暖かくしてね　あなた

一人になっても
あったかく生きて
ありがとう
おうちって言ってくれて

Home

When you were a baby
You stayed in a hospital for one month
In a sickness serious
Do you remember?
In the hospital you kept saying

"I'll be home! I don't like the hospital!"
When leaving the hospital you returned home
You looked around in our flat
Here and there
Do you remember?

Not having a hearth
Nor a mantelpiece
But a home
Your home this is

Sorry for you
Your mom sometimes missed cleaning it
But you see
Remember it
That you said, "I'll be home!"

It has an air-conditioner though
But spare energy cost and
Cover yourself thick with your bed covers
To keep you warm

If you should have to live alone
Live your life warm
Thank you at the time you said
"Home!"

(Tanslator: Noriko Mizusaki)

ひまわりへのオード

ひまわりのようにすっくと高く立ち
青空と夏の雲を背負っていたい　そして
夏の太陽に向かって　大きく開きたい
昼の風は軽くすこやかに渡って行くだろう

輝く夏の日
涼しい風が撫でて行く昼
黄金色のひまわり畑の脇を
息子と手を繋いで歩いて行きたい
どこまでも

息子よ
暗い日も　ひまわりのようであって欲しい
すこやかに笑い
すこやかに心開いて欲しい
太陽に向かって　大きく

Ode to the Sunflower

I want to stand straight up like a sunflower
carrying the blue sky and summer clouds on the back
blooming out big and wide up towards the sun in the summer
the wind in high noon will pass me lightly through

On a bright summer day
at noon cheerful winds would pass by caressing me
along beside the golden field of sunflowers
I want to walk with my son joining our hands together
on and on slowly but without any stops

My son!
I want you like the sunflower
even on darker days
laughing and
opening your mind wide
up towards the golden sun

(Translator: Noriko Mizusaki)

夏祭り

藍の浴衣に汗あおぐ
団扇の手をとめ
君と行く
舟に川風
流れて涼し

人生は
廻り灯籠のまぼろしよ
まわりまわって
出会い
別れる

覗きいて
千々さまざまの
万華鏡
変わり変わるは
わが人生のさま

太鼓あり打つは華やか
船橋音頭　踊り踊れば
提灯揺れる
夏の日遠く
夕闇にあかり

Summer Festival

In yukata kimono I feel cool
my hand pauses for a round fan
sliding down the river with you
on our boat the breezes blowing
fan us cool we floating on

Life is
circulating lanterns
rounding and rounding
we meet and
part

Peeped in
changes so many
a kaleidoscope does
changes and changes
just like our life

The drum rumbling
striking our festival music
when we dance together
lanterns above us swing
illuminated the evening

ガンジスの黎明

ガンジス
漆黒の未明
暗黒
漆黒

チラチラ
小さな灯火
揺れる
去る
離れる
近寄る

老女の顔
灯火に見える
蝋燭を渡す
小さな皿
花

老女の顔の
皺
皺の下の
眼
私も
灯火を
流す

聖なる河
ガンジスに
漆黒の闇の

Dawn; The Ganges

The Ganges
night
darkness
pitch-dark

flickering
gleam
small candle lights
swaying
departing off
separating from me
approaching

a brown face of
an old woman
can be seen in the candle lights
she handed a small dish to me
with a tiny candle fire
a tiny flower beside

wrinkles deep
on her face
eyes dark
under her wrinkles
I put my candle dish on the water
it started floating away
on the waves

onto the holy river
the Ganges
in the pitch darkness

無数の魂が
火が
花が
行く
流れる
流れ去る

やがて
白い
朝
黎明

世界の
夜明け

numberless souls
in candle lights
in flowers
go
floating
go
floating
then
no sight

soon
a white morning
dawn

beginning
of the world

お月さま

東京に
おつきさまいない
だれかが言った

このごろは
そうだと思い
下ばかり見た

でもね　今日
ふと見上げたら
おつきさまいた

あれは何？
大きな電灯？
おつきさま

おつきさま
しばし見上げて
感動の

あら立派
うさぎさんたち
まだお餅つき

がんばって
ついたお餅を
くださいね

東京に
おつきさまいる
今日は十五夜

Moon Watching Festival

Oh my celestial moon
every time looking you up I have an idea
where is steamed rice balls offered?
"eating is better than watching"
my usual crazy habit for the festival

Offering autumn flowers in a vase
I looked you up high in the heaven
those days far and gone now
when I was young and innocent
my heart was beating high

Oh my dear celestial moon
you holding rabbits lovely
still in the arms so tenderly
science or space shuttles
I have no business with them

My dear moon so celestial
even when watching and staring you
I cannot feel sad which is so strange
taste of elegance or subtle beauty
likely had escaped from me

What is that?
yes it is the moon
even in Tokyo even now
we have for sure the moon
it sitting high up there alone

a large city lamp

おつきさま
笑いをくれる
しあわせも

おつきさま
いつもだっこの
うさぎさん

今日はお月見
お団子並べ
お歌うたおう

注：日本語は俳句、英語は短歌の形式です。

Note: In Japanese, these poems were written in the haiku style, while in English, in the Tanka style.

春

春が揺れる
どこかで　誰かが
ブランコの歌

春のリボンが
ふんわり　ふわり
私の髪はリボン色

クローバー
そよ風吹けば
しあわせオペラ

Spring

Spring sways
Somewhere: someone
A song of swings

A ribbon of the spring
Flows gentle on the wind
My hair has the ribbon color

Clovers
When a breeze blows
An opera of happiness

力一杯走っていこう

力一杯走って行こう
学校校庭
かわっぷち
角の公園
どこでもいいさ
走ればいいのさ

いじめられたら走ってみよう
叱られたら走っていこう
カレキの道でも
広い道でも
力一杯
世界一周

Go Dash As Hard As You Can

Go dash as hard as you can
In a school yard
On an edge of the river
In a park at the corner
Any place is all right
Just you have to is dash and dash

If we were bullied let's dash out
If we were scolded let's go dash
On the way of wrecks
On a main road
As hard as you can
Dash around the world

(Translator:Noriko Mizusaki)

風車
<small>かざぐるま</small>

まわそ　まわそよ
風車
花子が泣いて
太郎が笑って

まわそ　まわそよ
風車
いつまでまわる
風車

鮮やか七色
赤　黄色
悲しい時も
嬉しい時も
いつでもまわそ
風車

まわそ　くるくる
まわそ　ぐるぐる
太郎が泣いて
花子が笑って

いつでもまわせ
風車
地球の回転　地球の自転
まわる　まわるよ　風車

縁日おじさん
ニコニコ笑顔
売れ行き上々
風車

Windmill in a Toy

Turn and turn around
A windmill in a toy
Hanako cries there
Taro laughs here

Turn and turn around
The windmill in a toy
How long will it turn ?
The windmill in a toy

Colorful in the seven colors
Red and yellow ones
When you sad
When you happy
Any time you turn it
The windmill in a toy

Wheel it round
Turn it around
Taro cries there
Hanako laughs here

Any time turn it
The windmill in a toy
The earth's rotation
It rotates: it turns around

The old toy seller in a fair
Smiles all in his face
They sell well: a good sale
Windmills in toys

(Translator: Noriko Mizusaki)

かたち

あなたがまあるいとき
わたしもまるい

あなたがしかくいとき
わたしもましかく

でもゆるしてね
ときには

あなたがまあるいとき
わたしはさんかく

Shapes

When you are round
I am also round

When you are square
I am also square

But forgive me
Sometimes
When you are roundy
I am triangle in the shape

(Translator: Noriko Mizusaki)

ヒロシマの折り鶴

ヒロシマの
空に折り鶴
飛んで行く
群をなし　群となり
一面空を覆い尽くして

鐘鳴らせ
平和の鐘を
空高らかに
鐘の音に乗り
折り鶴の飛ぶ

繰り返すな　ヒロシマの悲劇
繰り返すな　世界の悲惨
なぜに　人間は愛せない？
ただ　憎しみあるばかり？
なぜに　苦しまねばならない
小さな者たちが？

折り鶴が飛んで行く
子供達が折った
私達が折った
千代紙で
千代紙とは永遠の紙

今日　ヒロシマの空は
雲もなし
ヒロシマの空
二度と汚してはならぬ空

日本の空
世界の空

Paper Cranes in Hiroshima

In the sky of Hiroshima
cranes of folding paper flying
in tens and hundreds
in thousands
they cover the sky of Hiroshima

ring the bell for peace
to the sky high up
riding the sound
the paper cranes are flying on

no more Hiroshima
no more of miseries of the world
why cannot the earth be filled with love?
only hatred survives?
why do the small ones have to suffer?

paper cranes are flying
children and all of us
folded them with paper
named "chiyogami"
meaning paper for thousands generations

today in the sky of Hiroshima
now cloudless
the sky of Hiroshima
we will not have to pollute again

the sky of Japan
the sky of the world

言葉の花束：終わりに

新川和江・水崎野里子

みなさん！おばちゃんの詩を読んでくれてありがとう！
世界にはいろいろな子供たちと大人たちがいます。
すべてのひとびとがしあわせで楽しい毎日を過ごしているとは限りません。
病気や戦争に苦しんでいる人もいます。貧困や嵐や地震に苦しんでいるひともいます。
人生には苦しいことも楽しいこともあります。でも負けないでまっすぐしあわせに生きてください。希望をいつも持ってください。
このご本は日本のおばちゃん二人のあなた方世界の子供たちに贈る花束です。

2018年秋

A Bouquet of Poems to you : After Words

Kazue Shinkawa & Noriko Mizusaki

Hi! All of you! Thanks for your reading our poems to the last one!
In the world various children and adults are living along.
But it is not that all of us are always living happy and merry days.
Some of us suffer from sickness or wars. Some people live in hardships from poverty and the natural disasters like storms and quakes.
You have to live through difficulties and hardships, while you can have a right to live in happiness.
Do not get defeated by them and live straight and in happiness. Always you do not forget hope.
We are two aunties living in Japan. This book is our present to you, all the children in the world, for peace and hope: A Bouquet of Poems to you.

Autumn, 2018

謝辞

このご本を刊行するにあたって、まず新川和江さまに感謝申し上げたい。ついでご本つくりと出版を了承いただいたブックウェイ出版社、黒田さんに感謝申し上げたい。

マザー・グースなど童話詩、子供のための詩というジャンルは新しくはないし世界中で多数書かれている。それは知っている。西条八十や北原白秋の「赤い鳥」などは日本の童謡と童話詩を基礎付けた。西条八十の弟子であった金子みすゞ、新川和江にならい、私もここでその道を歩ませていただいた。皆様、よろしくお願いします。

水崎野里子
2018年秋

Words of Gratitude

For the publication of this book, I would like to thank Kazue Shinkawa, at first. and then Ms. Kuroda, an editor of the publisher.

The genre of the children's verses are rather so popular and so productive in the English speaking countries, like "Mother Goose", which I know. In Japan, it is the same to us, but I like here in this book to express a special gratitude to the old and traditional legacies of "the Red Birds Magazine", published in Japan. It was led by Yaso Saijyo and Hakusyu Kitahara, etc, and they propagated children poems and songs, in the modern ages of Japan.

I also like to express special gtatitudes to the late Japanese poetess Misuzu Kaneko, together with Kazue Shinkawa, both of whom were directed by Yaso Saijyo.

In addition, here I express my gratitude to all of you I met so far, including you readers of this tiny book. Thanks.

Noriko Mizusaki
In the autumn, 2018.

日本女性２人詩集（１）　おばさんから子どもたちへ　贈る詩の花束

2018年10月11日　発行

著　者　新川和江、水崎野里子

発行所　ブックウェイ

〒670-0933　姫路市平野町62
TEL.079 (222) 5372　FAX.079 (244) 1482
https://bookway.jp

印刷所　小野高速印刷株式会社

©Kazue Shinkawa, Noriko Mizusaki 2018,

Printed in Japan

ISBN978-4-86584-351-4

乱丁本・落丁本は送料小社負担でお取り換えいたします。

本書のコピー、スキャン、デジタル化等の無断複製は著作権法上での例外を除き
禁じられています。本書を代行業者等の第三者に依頼してスキャンやデジタル化
することは、たとえ個人や家庭内の利用でも一切認められておりません。